monday morning®

Super-Duper Science
Twinkle, Twinkle

by Annalisa Suid
illustrated by Marilynn G. Barr

For Susie Fisch

Publisher: Roberta Suid
Editor: Carol Whiteley
Design & Production: Susan Pinkerton
Educational Consultant: Sarah Felstiner
Cover Art: Mike Artell

Also by the author: *Save the Animals!* (MM 1964), *Love the Earth!* (MM 1965), *Learn to Recycle!* (MM 1966), *Sing A Song About Animals* (MM 1987), and *Preschool Connections* (MM 1993).

On-line address: MMBooks@AOL.com

CONTENTS

INTRODUCTION

Twinkle, Twinkle is composed of seven chapters, each a complete unit dedicated to a specific space theme. This book is intended to help children develop a hands-on understanding of science and to relate to the universe in a personal way: learning through games, observations, literature, and art.

The **Let's Read** section of each chapter features a popular children's book, such as *Goodnight Moon* by Margaret Wise Brown, and is accompanied by a detailed plot description. **Let's Talk** helps children link the featured book with familiar feelings, thoughts, or ideas in their own lives. For example, in the sun chapter, the "Let's Talk" discussion focuses on morning rituals.

Let's Learn is filled with facts. For example, the sun is a star, and only a medium-hot one at that. Choose facts that you think will interest your children, or copy the facts onto a sheet and post it in the room. Read a fact a day during the unit, or distribute fact sheets to parents so they can support their child's learning at home.

The **Let's Create** activities in each chapter allow children to use their imaginations. They will put together sundials, planet mobiles, shooting-star murals, Saturn-ring hats, and so on.

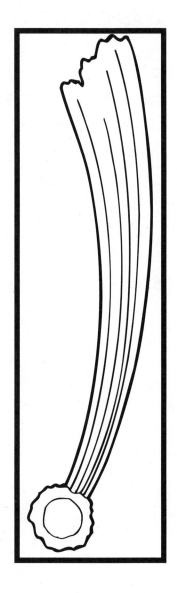

Children make a hands-on science connection as they engage in the **Let's Find Out** activities. These projects focus on exploration, leading children through moments of discovery as they find out what it's like to land on the red planet or what really happens to the moon during its cycle.

Let's Play suggests a new game (or games) to interest children in the theme of the chapter. A chant or a new song sung to a familiar tune is featured in the **Let's Sing** section. Children can learn the new lyrics and perform them for other classes, parents, or each other. Mother Goose rhymes are also included if there's a rhyme that fits the particular chapter.

Informative **Pattern Pages** complete each chapter. These patterns can be duplicated (reduced or enlarged) and used to decorate a bulletin board display. Make additional copies for the children to color using crayons or markers.

At the end of the book, you'll find a **Storybook Resources** section filled with additional fiction picture- and storybooks, plus a **Nonfiction Resources** section suggesting factual and photograph books of the featured space topics.

ALL ABOUT SPACE

STARS:
Stars are huge balls of hot, glowing gases. Astronomers are not really sure why stars twinkle. They think it is because the Earth's air is moving. When light from the stars passes through moving air, the stars appear to twinkle.

MOON:
The moon is our nearest neighbor in space. It seems bigger and brighter than the stars, but really it is much smaller. It only seems bigger because it is so much closer to us than any star. There is no water or air on the moon. Our moon travels around the Earth, just as the Earth travels around the sun.

SUN:
The sun is a star. Of all the stars, the sun is closest to us. Because it is near, it seems to be the brightest and the biggest star in the sky. But it isn't. It is really only a medium-sized star.

PLANETS:
Mercury is the closest planet to the sun. Apart from the moon, Venus is the brightest object in the night sky. Mars is known as the red planet. One thousand Earths could fit inside Jupiter! Saturn's rings are made of objects ranging in size from "dust" particles to boulders about 30 feet across. Uranus and Neptune each have diameters nearly four times that of Earth. Pluto is the smallest planet.

COMETS:
A comet has an icy core and is covered by a layer of black dust. As a comet orbits closer to the sun, the ice begins to change from a solid to a gas. The gas carries away some of the dust particles and spreads out around the nucleus in a large cloud called a coma.

METEORS:
Meteors begin as bits of rock or metal that orbit around the sun. But sometimes they plunge into Earth's atmosphere. The friction makes them glow red-hot, and they are then called meteors.

MILKY WAY:
The Milky Way is only one galaxy among millions of others in the universe. Galaxies are found in every part of the universe.

STARS

Introduction

★ Let's Read:

Draw Me a Star by Eric Carle (Philomel, 1992).
"Draw me a star. And the artist drew a star. It was a good star.
Draw me a sun, said the star. And the artist drew a sun...." This
beautifully illustrated story continues until the world is
complete, with moon, people, rainbows, animals, and more.
At the end of the book, step-by-step directions show how to
draw a star.

★ Let's Talk:

Lead children through the step-by-step instructions for
drawing a star, or duplicate the "I'm a Star" pattern (p. 18) for
children to decorate. Hang the completed stars from
different lengths of string or yarn around the room. Then let
children make a wish upon their stars. If they'd like, children
can add other creations from the book: the sun, moon, and
so on.

★ Let's Learn:

On a clear night, you can see between 1,500 and 2,000 stars.
However, astronomers believe that the number of stars in the
universe is about 200 quintillion (200 billion billion). People
have always looked at the stars and seen pictures in the
night sky. These pictures, which work like "connect the dots"
drawings, are called constellations. Constellations take many
different shapes: a goat, crab, ladle (dipper), hunter, and
more.

Let's Create: Twinkle, Twinkle, Little Star

Teach children the Mother Goose rhyme (p. 17), and its accompanying, less-well-known verse.

★ What You Need:

Construction paper (black or dark blue), glue (in squeeze bottles or in small cups with cotton swabs for dabbing), gold or silver glitter, newsprint, pastel crayons

★ What You Do:

1. Cover the work area with newsprint to protect it (and to catch excess glitter).
2. Let children make star patterns on their papers using the glue. Or they can just make dots to look like far-off stars.
3. Show the children how to sprinkle the glitter onto their papers and then carefully shake the excess off. (Gather this up at the end of the activity and save for another project.)
4. Provide pastel crayons for children to use to create additional decorations on their papers.
5. Post the completed pictures on a "Starry, Starry Night" bulletin board.

Book Link:

• *Stars* by Seymour Simon (William Morris, 1986). This is a photographic nonfiction book with great pictures to show kids and facts for adults' use.

Let's Find Out: About Pictures in the Sky

Many cultures have seen "pictures in the sky." These constellations are known by different names according to the designs, people, or animals seen.

★ What You Need:
Constellation patterns (pp. 10-11), blue construction paper, black markers

★ What You Do:
1. Describe the constellations to the children as pictures in the sky. They might be able to understand this image better if you compare the constellations to dot-to-dot pictures.
2. Duplicate and enlarge the constellation patterns. Have children draw a picture around each constellation pattern.
3. Provide blue construction paper and black markers for children to create their own constellations. They can make dots on a page representing a picture, and then hand the page to another child to connect the dots.

Book Links:
• *Find the Constellations* by H.A. Rey, revised edition (Houghton Mifflin, 1976). This resource helps to find the pictures in the sky by connecting the dots within the constellations. Informative for adults or for older children.
• *The Glow-in-the-dark Zodiac* by Katherine Ross, illustrated by Stephen Marchesi (Random House, 1993). Shows the pictures from the zodiac and gives background information.

~ CONSTELLATION PATTERNS ~

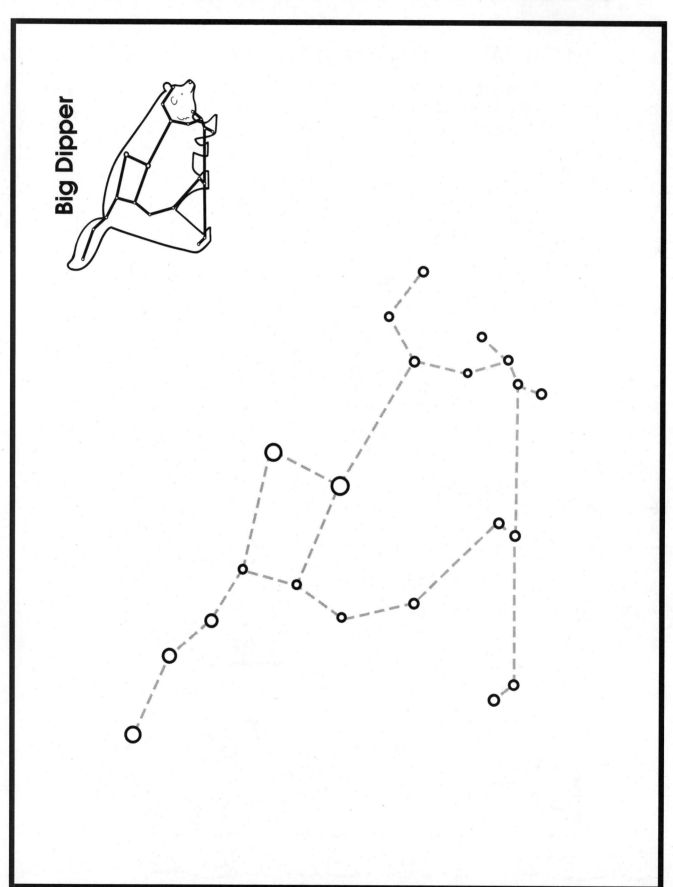

Big Dipper

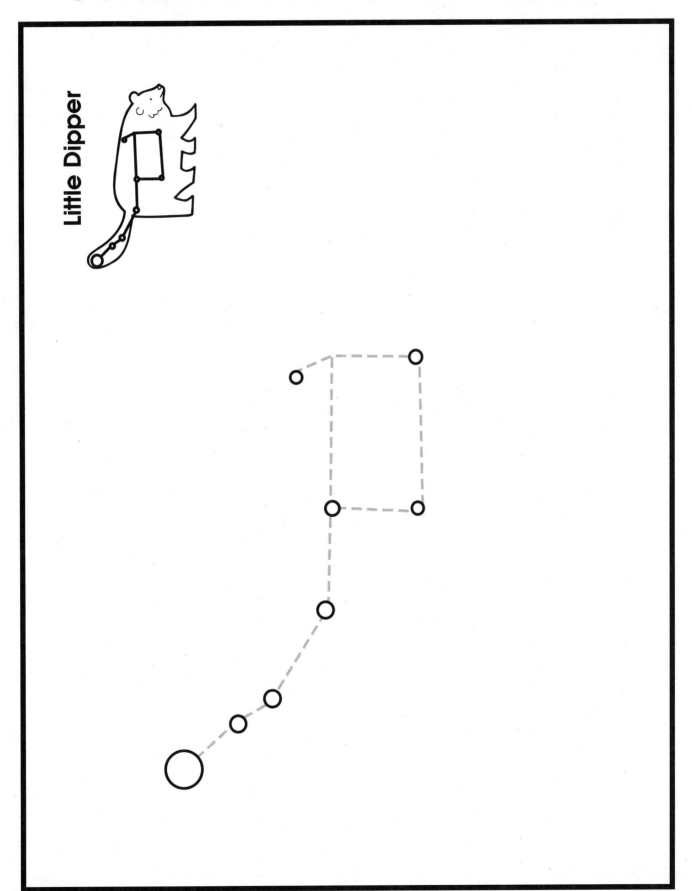

Little Dipper

Let's Find Out: Where Stars Go in the Daytime

Actually, stars don't go anywhere in the daytime. However, in the daytime, the light from the sun is so bright that you cannot see the light coming from the other stars.

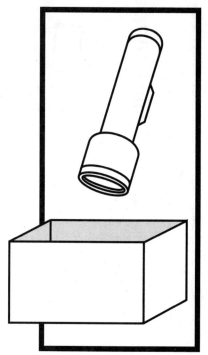

★ What You Need:
Shoe box, flashlight, pin

★ What You Do:
1. Use the pin to poke holes in the bottom of the shoe box.
2. Keeping the classroom light on, have the children sit on the floor around you. Shine the flashlight into the shoe box, so that the light comes through the holes.
3. Ask the children if it is easy or hard to see the light.
4. Turn off the classroom lights and lower the curtains until it is dark in the room.
5. Try the experiment again, asking whether it is easier or harder to see the flashlight when the room is dark.
6. Explain that the stars are always in the sky, but when the sun is out, it's too bright to see them. When it's dark, the light from the stars is much easier to see.

Book Link:
• *All About Stars* by Lawrence Jeffries (Troll, 1983). A "Question and Answer" Book that answers such questions as "Why do stars twinkle?"

Let's Play: Twinkle, Twinkle

★ What You Need:
Game board pattern (p. 14), game card patterns (p. 15), crayons or felt pens, scissors, game markers (for children's use), laminator

★ What You Do:
1. Duplicate the game board pattern, color as desired, laminate, and cut out again, leaving at least an 1/8" border so edges stay sealed. (You may enlarge this pattern, if desired.)
2. Duplicate the game cards, color as desired, laminate, and cut out.
3. Show children how to play this game. They pick a card and then move their marker to the matching square on the game board.
4. The first child to reach the twinkling star wins.

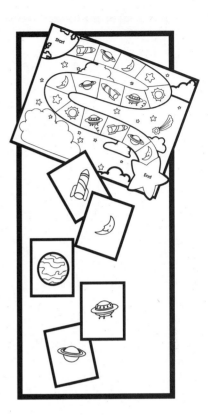

GAME BOARD PATTERN

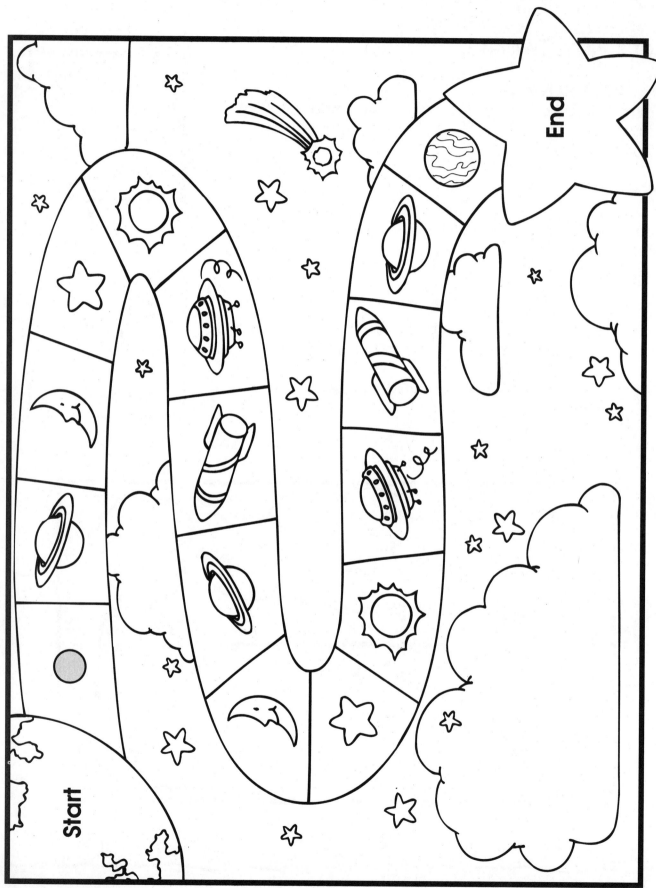

Start

End

14

GAME CARD PATTERNS

STARS

Let's Sing: Star Songs

A Star Is Bright

(to the tune of "Miss Mary Mack")

A star is bright, bright, bright.
It shines at night, night, night.
It glows just right, right, right.
It's out of sight, sight, sight!

A Star Makes an Excellent Night Light

(to the tune of "My Bonnie Lies Over the Ocean")

A star makes an excellent night light,
A star keeps the moon company—
A star, when it twinkles, is so bright,
Oh, star, won't you twinkle for me, for me?

Twinkle, oh, twinkle,
Oh, twinkle your bright light for me, for me.
Twinkle, oh, twinkle,
Oh, twinkle your bright light for me.

STARS

Let's Learn: Mother Goose Rhymes

Twinkle, Twinkle, Little Star

Twinkle, twinkle, little star,
How I wonder what you are.
Up above the world so high,
Like a diamond in the sky.
Twinkle, twinkle, little star,
How I wonder what you are.

When the blazing sun has gone,
When he nothing shines upon,
Then you show your little light.
Twinkle, twinkle, through the night.

Star Light, Star Bright

Star light, star bright,
The first star I see tonight.
I wish I may, I wish I might,
Have the wish I wish tonight.

"I'M A STAR"

MOON

Introduction

★ Let's Read:

Goodnight Moon by Margaret Wise Brown, pictures by Clement Hurd (HarperCollins, 1947).

"In the great green room, there was a telephone, and a red balloon, and a picture of the cow jumping over the moon." And there was also a little bunny, who said goodnight to each and every object in the room before he went to sleep. (Have the children look for the little mouse that hides on each two-page color spread!)

★ Let's Talk:

Ask your children if they have any bedtime rituals that they follow before going to sleep. For example, do they have a drink of water? Or do they turn on their night light? Have the children share their "before bedtime" schedules. Then, before nap time (if appropriate), say goodnight to the objects in the room.

★ Let's Learn:

The moon moves around the Earth. As it does, different parts of it are lit by the sun. When the moon is on the opposite side of the Earth from the sun, the side we see is completely lit. We call this the "full moon."

Let's Create: Moon Faces

★ What You Need:
Face paints, mirrors, Mother Goose moon rhymes (pp. 30-31)

★ What You Do:
1. Read the Mother Goose moon rhymes with the children.
2. Discuss the way the moon looks when it's full. Ask the children if they can see a face on the moon when they look at it.
3. Provide face paints in yellow and white for children to use to make moon faces on their own faces.
4. Set up mirrors for children to use as they paint their own faces.

Option: Take photos of your children's moon faces and bind them in a "Celestial Photo Album."

Let's Create: A Marvelous Moon Mobile

Recite "Hey, Diddle, Diddle" with the children
before embarking on this activity.

Hey, Diddle, Diddle

Hey, diddle, diddle,
The cat and the fiddle,
The cow jumped over the moon.
The little dog laughed, to see such sport,
And the dish ran away with the spoon.

★ What You Need:

Hey, Diddle, Diddle patterns (pp. 22-23), heavy paper, crayons
or markers, scissors, hole punch, yarn, tape, wire clothes
hangers (one per child)

★ What You Do:

1. Duplicate the patterns onto heavy paper and cut out. Make
a set for each child. (Older children will be able to cut out the
patterns themselves.)
2. Let children color the patterns using crayons or markers.
Remind them to color both sides, since both sides of the
patterns will be seen.
3. Have the children punch holes in the appropriate parts of
the patterns.
4. Show children how to thread lengths of yarn through the
holes.
5. Help the children attach the patterns to the hanger by tying
or taping the yarn lengths to the wire.

Option: Children can cover the body of the hanger with
colored construction paper or fabric.

HEY, DIDDLE, DIDDLE PATTERNS

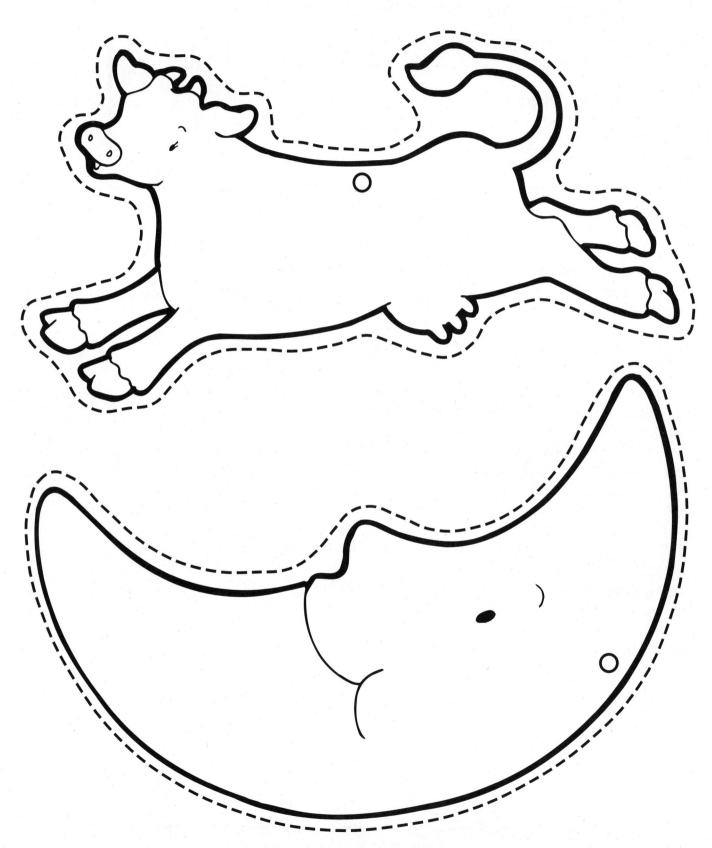

HEY, DIDDLE, DIDDLE PATTERNS

MOON

Let's Find Out: About Moon Phases

Have children observe the moon at night when they are home with their families before doing this activity. Ask parents or guardians to look at the moon with their children.

★ What You Need:
Window pattern (p. 25), moon cards (p. 28) or moon pictures, crayons or markers (especially yellow, gold, or silver), star stickers (optional)

★ What You Do:
1. Duplicate the window pattern. Make one for each child.
2. Show children pictures of the moon in its different phases in one of the nonfiction resources listed at the end of this book. You can also use the moon cards from "Ask Mr. Moon."
3. Tell children that a long time ago, people used the moon as a calendar. They noted the passing of time by the changes the moon went through.
4. In each pane of the window pattern have children draw one phase of the moon: full, half, quarter, and new.
5. Provide star stickers for children to use to further decorate their night sky pictures.
6. Bind the pictures into a cooperative "Goodbye Moon" book.

Book Links:
• *Papa, Please Get the Moon for Me* by Eric Carle (Picture Book Studio, 1986). Monica's father tries to bring the moon home to her, but the moon is too big. Luckily, the moon gets smaller every night, and when it is small enough Papa takes it back to Monica.
• *The Moon Seems to Change* (rev. edition) by Franklyn M. Branley, illustrated by Barbara and Ed Emberly (Crowell, 1987). This "Let's-Read-and-Find-Out" science book explains the phases of the moon—the changes that seem to happen as it goes around Earth.

WINDOW PATTERN

Let's Find Out: About Moon Rocks

★ What You Need:
Pebbles (preferably smooth ones), tempera paints, paintbrushes, newsprint, sandbox or sand table

★ What You Do:
1. Cover the working area with newsprint.
2. Give each child a pebble to paint with the tempera paint.
3. Let the pebbles dry.
4. Have children place their pebbles in the sandbox or in a sand table.
5. Let children pretend to be astronauts on the moon, discovering the moon rocks for the first time. They can pick up the rocks and pretend that they are bringing them back to Earth.

Option: To make glittery rocks, let children paint over the pebbles with glue, then shake them in a glitter-filled zip-closure bag. Let dry.

Book Links:
• *Rocks from Space* by Richard O. Norton (Mountain Press, 1974).
• *The Old Man and the Astronauts: A Melanesian Tale*, written and edited by Ruth Tabrah, illustrated by George Suyeoka (Island Heritage, 1975).

Let's Play: Ask Mr. Moon

★ **What You Need:**
Moon cards (p. 28), crayons or markers, scissors, clear Contac paper or laminator (optional)

★ **What You Do:**
1. Duplicate the cards twice, color if desired, laminate (or cover with clear Contac paper), and cut out. For best results, cut cards apart before laminating, laminate, and cut out again. Otherwise the edges tend to peel up. (If children are playing for four of a kind, make four copies of the cards.)
2. Teach children how to play the game. It is similar to "Go Fish." The cards are shuffled and dealt to the children playing. Each child might get four–six cards (depending on their abilities). They are playing for matches of two or four, again depending on their abilities. One child will ask another, "Do you have a full moon?" If yes, that child hands the card over to the first child, who now has a match and can lay the cards down. If not, the child asked says, "Ask Mr. Moon," and the other child must draw a card from the remaining cards in the deck. The object is for the player to make the most matches and get rid of all the cards in his or her hand.

Option: Color code the moons so that children can ask, "Do you have any red moons?" if they don't remember the words for "full moon," "quarter moon," and so on.

MOON CARDS

MOON

Let's Sing: Moon Songs

I See the Full Moon

(to the tune of "He's Got the Whole World in His Hands")

I see the full moon, in the sky,
I see the full, round moon, in the sky,
I see the full moon, in the sky,
I see the full moon in the sky!

The Moon's Not Made of Cheese

(to the tune of "The Farmer in the Dell")

The moon's not made of cheese,
The moon's not made of cheese,
It's big and white and shines at night,
But it's not made of cheese!

When I Am Lying in My Bed

(to the tune of "The Ants Go Marching One by One")

When I am lying in my bed
At night, at night,
The moon shines down from overhead,
So bright, so bright.
When I am lying in my bed,
The moon shines down from overhead
And it makes my room so bright,
In the night, with its pale moonlight.
(Shine, shine, shine!)

Let's Learn: Mother Goose Rhymes

The Man in the Moon Came Down Too Soon

The man in the moon came down too soon
To inquire the way to Norridge.
The man in the south, he burnt his mouth
With eating cold plum porridge.

The Man in the Moon Looked Out

The man in the moon
Looked out of the moon,
And this is what he said,
'Tis time that, now I'm getting up,
All babies went to bed.

Sippity Sup, Sippity Sup

Sippity sup, sippity sup,
Bread and milk from a china cup,
Bread and milk from a bright silver spoon,
Made from a piece of the bright silver moon!
Sippity sup, sippity sup, sippity, sippity sup!

What's the News of the Day?

What's the news of the day,
Good neighbor, I pray?
They say the balloon
Is gone up to the moon.

Let's Learn: Mother Goose Rhymes

There Was an Old Woman

There was an old woman
Tossed up in a basket,
Nineteen times as high as the moon.
Where she was going
I couldn't but ask it,
For under her arm she carried a broom.

"Old woman, old woman, old woman,"
    cried I.
"Where are you going to up so high?"
"To sweep the cobwebs out of the sky."
"Shall I come with you?"
"Aye, by and by."

On Saturday Night

On Saturday night, I lost my wife,
And where do you think I found her?
Up in the moon, singing a tune,
And all the stars around her.

I See the Moon

I see the moon
And the moon sees me;
God bless the moon
And God bless me.

"I'M THE MOON"

SUN

Introduction

★ Let's Read:

Who Gets the Sun Out of Bed? by Nancy White Carlstrom, illustrated by David McPhail (Little, 1992).
On a cold winter morning, the lazy sun is reluctant to rise. Who will wake him up? The moon tries, and so does a bunny named Midnight and a little boy named Nicholas. Finally, all three together succeed.

★ Let's Talk:

Ask your children who gets *them* out of bed. Do they wake up on their own; with the help of an alarm clock; or do their parents, guardians, or siblings get them up? Discuss early morning schedules: bathing and dressing routines, breakfast schedules, and so on. Children can compare their situations from household to household. (See *The Way to Start a Day* in **Nonfiction Resources**. This book describes how people all over the world celebrate the sunrise.)

★ Let's Learn:

The sun is a star, just one among the billions in our galaxy. It looks bigger than the other stars in the sky because we are closer to it. If the sun were a hollow ball, over a million Earths could be put inside it. Very hot stars are blue to bluish white. Cooler stars have a dull red color. The sun is a medium-hot star.

Let's Create: A Sunny Day

Discuss the fact that on sunny days, people need to protect themselves from the hot rays of the sun. In Australia, they call this "Slip, slop, and slap," referring to slipping on a shirt, slopping on some sunscreen, and slapping on a hat before going outside!

★ **What You Need:**
Sunny day patterns (p. 35), construction paper, scissors, crayons or markers, glue

★ **What You Do:**
1. Duplicate the sunny day patterns for each child. Cut out the patterns or let children do this themselves.
2. Discuss the different things people like to do on sunny days: go to the beach, have a picnic, go to the park, ride a bike, go swimming, and so on. Then talk about the different ways people can protect themselves from the sun's rays.
3. Provide construction paper for the backgrounds, and let children use crayons or markers to draw sunny day scenes on their papers.
4. Children can color and glue on the patterns to show the items that can be used for protection on sunny days.

Option 1: Let children use gold foil to make shining suns on their papers.

Option 2: Play "sunny" music while children work, such as, "Here Comes the Sun" and "Good Day Sunshine" (Beatles) or "Sunny Days" (Sesame Street theme song).

SUNNY DAY PATTERNS

Let's Find Out: About Shadows

Remind children about the story of Peter Pan. In it, Peter loses his shadow, which Mary graciously sews back on for him. Tell the children that they can't lose their shadows, then challenge them to go outside and find them!

★ What You Need:
Sunlight

★ What You Do:
1. Take the children outside on a sunny afternoon.
2. Have them try to find their shadows.
3. Once they succeed, challenge them to try to outsmart their shadows: Can they run faster than their shadows? Can they lose their shadows?
4. Take the children into a shady area and have them see if their shadows stay with them.

Option: Take children outside during different parts of the day. In the morning, their shadows will be longer than at noontime, and their noontime shadows will be going in a different direction. Shadows change as the height of the sun in the sky changes. As the sun becomes higher, shadows are shorter. Then, as the sun sinks lower in the sky, shadows get longer.

Book Links:
• *Shadow Magic* by Seymour Simon, illustrated by Stella Ormai (Lothrop, 1985). This book explains what shadows are and how they are formed. It also tells how to make a sundial and a shadow show.
• *In Shadowland* by Mitsumasa Anno (Orchard, 1988). "Suppose there was a land of shadows," begins this book. Supposing there is one, Anno has certainly captured it!

Let's Find Out: About Sundials

Discuss the concepts of clocks and telling time. Ask if any of the children knows a way to tell time without a clock...the sun! Remember, sundials only work when the sun is shining!

★ What You Need:
Sundial pattern (p. 38), modeling clay or playdough, straws or Popsicle sticks, crayons

★ What You Do:
1. Duplicate the sundial pattern for each child in the classroom.
2. Give each child a little bit of clay to form into a small lump.
3. Take the children outside.
4. Have the children set their sundial patterns on the ground in a sunny area.
5. Have the children place their lump of clay in the center of the sundial pattern.
6. Give each child a straw or Popsicle stick to stick in the center of the clay ball.
7. Have the children observe the shadow that the sun creates on their paper. They can mark the shadow with a crayon.
8. Take the children outside a few times during the day and have them see if the shadow has moved. (They can mark the movement with their crayons.)

Book Links:
• *A Choice of Sundials* by Winthrop W. Dolan (S. Greene Press, 1975).
• *Sun Calendar* by Una Jacobs (Silver Burdett, 1983).
• *Our Planet Earth* by Robert Estalella, illustrated by Marcel Socias (Barron's Educational Series, 1994). Includes directions for making a sundial.

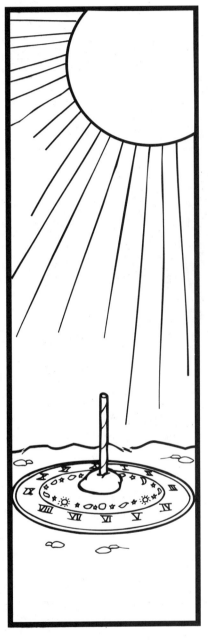

SUNDIAL PATTERN

Let's Play: Shadow Tag

★ **What You Need:**
Sunlight, space to run outside

★ **What You Do:**
1. Have the children go outside and find their shadows.
2. Choose one child to be "It." This child tries to tag the other children by stepping on their shadows.
3. Have the children "freeze" when tagged. They can try to hold still enough to keep their shadow the same.
4. The last child to be tagged becomes "It" in the next round.

Let's Sing: Sunny Songs

I'm a Little Sun Ray

(to the tune of "I'm a Little Teapot")

I'm a little sun ray,
I'm so bright—
I can make you warm
With my gold light.
When you go outside
With friends to play...
I'll be there
On sunny days!

It's So Sunny

(to the tune of "Alouette")

It's so sunny,
Yes, it is so sunny.
It's so sunny,
And the sky is blue.
When the sun is shining bright,
We can play in the sunlight.
Shining bright,
Shining bright,
The sunlight,
The sunlight,
Ohhhhh.
It's so sunny,
Yes, it is so sunny.
It's so sunny,
And the sky is blue!

SUN

Let's Learn: Mother Goose Rhymes

For All the Evil Under the Sun

For all the evil under the sun,
There is a remedy, or there is none.
If there be one, try and find it;
If there be none, never mind it.

A Sunshiny Shower

A sunshiny shower
Won't last half an hour.

"I'M THE SUN"

PLANETS

Introduction

★ Let's Read:

Babar Visits Another Planet by Laurent de Brunhoff (Random House, 1972).
Babar and his family are kidnapped and taken to a strange planet where other creatures, who look similar to elephants, provide them with a variety of adventures. Babar, Celeste, and their children have a pleasant visit, and then return home.

★ Let's Talk:

Hold a discussion about traveling. Ask if your children have ever been to a place that seemed strange to them. If so, ask the reasons why, for example, if they visited another part of the country, people might have spoken with unusual accents; if they visited a different country, people might have spoken in another language. Have the children brainstorm reasons why foreigners might find the United States to be strange!

★ Let's Learn:

Stars stay in the same part of the sky, but planets are always moving. Planets move around the sun. Most planets would not be good to live on. Mercury and Venus are too hot. Mars is too cold and covered with red dust. Jupiter, Saturn, Uranus, Neptune, and Pluto are also cold...but Earth is just right!

Let's Create: Ring-a-Ring-'Round-Saturn Visors

Teach the children the song to the tune of "Ring-Around-the-Rosie" (p. 50) before making these super Saturn hats.

★ What You Need:
Paper plates (one per child), scissors, tempera paints in a variety of colors, paintbrushes, newsprint, craft knife (optional)

★ What You Do:
1. Cut out a paper plate ring (or band) by folding the plate in half and cutting out the center circle. Leave the ring intact. Make one ring for each child. Or use a craft knife to cut out the central portion. (You may want to experiment with the size of the circles you cut out, depending on the head size of the children in your class.)
2. Provide multi-colored tempera paints for children to use to paint circles around their paper plate ring. They can try painting circular stripes all the way around for authentic rings.
3. Let the rings dry.
4. Have the children wear their Saturn-ring visors on sunny days.

Book Links:
• *Saturn: The Spectacular Planet* by Franklyn M. Branley, illustrated by Leonard Kessler (Crowell, 1983). Factual with black and white drawings and a few four-color photographs.
• *Saturn* by Don Davis and Ian Halliday (BLA, 1989). Factual with beautiful four-color photographs to show children.

Let's Create: 3-D Red, Red Planet

Mars is a cold planet that is covered with red dust. If possible, show your children pictures of Mars from books listed in **Nonfiction Resources**.

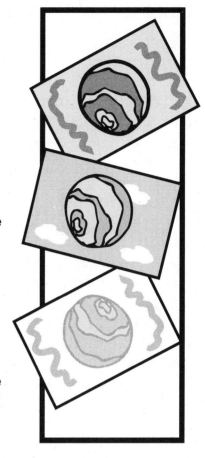

★ What You Need:
Colored sand (red), Mars pattern (p. 51), construction paper, glue, scissors, crayons or markers, star stickers (optional)

★ What You Do:
1. Enlarge and duplicate the Mars pattern and cut out. Make one for each child. (Older children will be able to cut out the pattern themselves.)
2. Provide construction paper for children to use as backgrounds for their pictures.
3. Let children glue their Mars pattern to the construction paper and paint the pattern with a thin layer of glue.
4. Provide colored sand for children to sprinkle on their Mars pattern. (You can mix dry red tempera with dry sand, or have the children swirl small cups of sand with a piece of red chalk to make red sand. Red glitter is another option.)
5. Provide crayons and markers for children to use to decorate the rest of the picture.
6. If desired, let children add star stickers to make their pictures sparkle.

Let's Create: Playdough Planets

Show children color pictures of the planets before embarking on this activity.

★ What You Need:
"We Are the Planets" patterns (pp. 51-52), playdough in a variety of colors, crayons or markers, small plate to hold each child's solar system collection

★ What You Do:
1. Enlarge and duplicate the planetary patterns. Color if desired.
2. Provide children with playdough in enough colors that they can use a different color for each planet. Or let the children mix colors to get swirly Earth-like effects (blue/white/green).
3. Set out the planet patterns for children to look at. Have them make planets from their playdough. (If you've colored the patterns, you can have children make playdough planets in the same colors.)
4. Help the children name each of their planets. (You don't need to write these down. You can simply have the children hold up their finished planets as you call out the names.)
5. Write the children's names on their plates, where they can keep and display their Solar Systems.

PLANETS

Let's Create: Coop-planetary Mobiles

These mobiles are cooperative efforts by groups of children.

★ What You Need:

"We Are the Planets" patterns (pp. 51-52), scissors, crayons or markers (including black), hole punch, yarn, hangers

★ What You Do:

1. Enlarge and duplicate the planet patterns and cut out.
2. Give each child one or two planets to decorate with crayons or markers. Have the children color both sides of the patterns.
3. Write the name of each planet on the pattern.
4. Punch a hole in each pattern and thread with yarn.
5. Fasten the yarn to the hanger to make each mobile. Make sure you use only one of each planet for each mobile.
6. Hang the "Coop-planetary Mobiles" around the room.

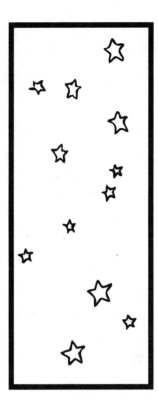

PLANETS

Let's Find Out: About Planet Placement

Children will be interested in learning which planets are close to the sun, which are far away, and which are just right to live on—only Earth!

★ **What You Need:**
"We Are the Planets" patterns (pp. 51-52), crayons or markers, clear Contac paper, glue or tape

★ **What You Do:**
1. Duplicate the planet patterns for each child.
2. Have the children color the patterns using crayons or markers. Go over the names of the planets, and the order in which the planets appear. Point out which planets are too hot to live on (Mercury and Venus), which are too cold (all after Earth), and which is just right (Earth).
3. Glue or tape the colored patterns together.
4. Cover the completed patterns with clear Contac paper.
5. Let the children use their planet placement patterns for place mats at snack time. Or they can take them home and use them at meals with their families.

Let's Play: Planet Matching

★ What You Need:
"We Are the Planets" patterns (pp. 51-52), crayons or markers, tape, laminator or clear Contac paper, scissors

★ What You Do:
1. Duplicate the patterns.
2. Color each planet a different color.
3. Attach the two pages with tape and cover the entire game board with clear Contac paper.
4. Make a separate copy of the planet patterns and cut out each planet.
5. Color the planet patterns to match the colors on the game board. (Laminate or cover with clear Contac paper if desired, then cut out again.)
6. Let children take turns placing the planets in the appropriate spots. They will be able to match both sizes and colors.
7. When a child has matched all of the planets, check the work and then let another child take a turn.

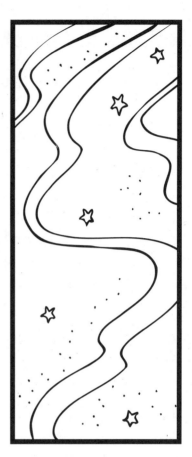

PLANETS

Let's Sing: Planet Songs

Ring-a-Ring 'Round Saturn
(to the tune of "Ring-Around-the-Rosie")

Ring-a-ring 'round Saturn,
The rings are in a pattern,
Ice and rocks, they all go 'round!

Planet Mars
(to the tune of "London Bridge Is Falling Down")

Planet Mars is cold and red,
Cold and red,
Cold and red.
Planet Mars is cold and red,
I can't live there!

Planet Earth is nice and green,
Nice and green,
Nice and green.
Planet Earth is nice and green,
I can live here!

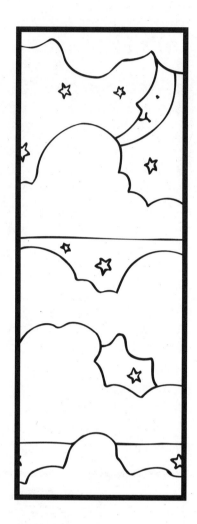

Mercury's Too Hot
(to the tune of "The Farmer in the Dell")

Mercury's too hot,
Yes, Mercury's too hot,
I wouldn't want to live there,
Because Mercury's too hot.

But Earth is just the place,
In all of outer space.
I'm glad we live on planet Earth,
With the whole human race!

"WE ARE THE PLANETS"

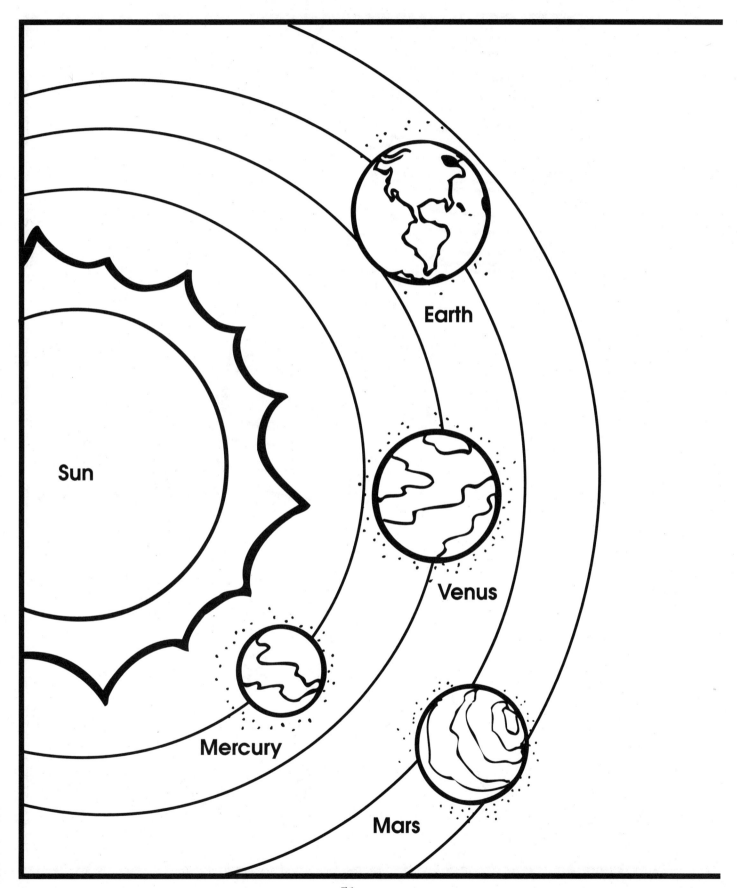

"WE ARE THE PLANETS"

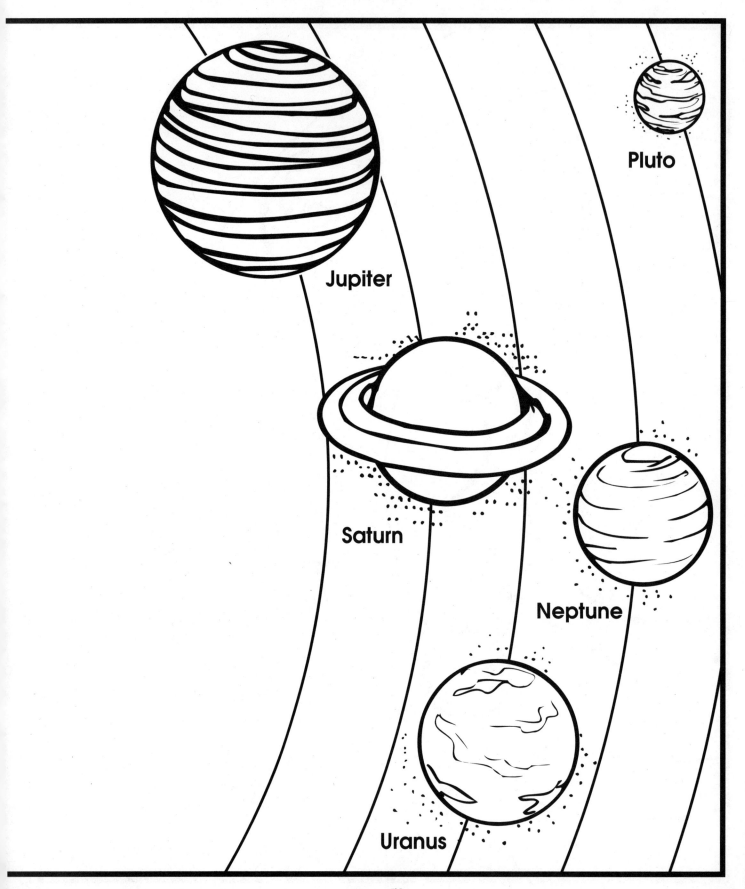

Pluto

Jupiter

Saturn

Neptune

Uranus

COMETS & METEORS

Introduction

★ Let's Read:
Meteor! by Patricia Polacco (Dodd, 1987).
A quiet, rural community is drastically changed when a meteor crashes in the front yard of the Gaw family's house. The landing of the "shooting star" excites everyone! People in town decide that simply being near the meteor (or even touching it) helps them to do anything better, like playing the trumpet!

★ Let's Talk:
Ask your children to list reasons why they are special: they can tie their shoes, use silverware, ride a trike, and so on. Then ask if they think there is anything that could make them do these activities better. Do they think that touching a meteor could improve their skills? Have them brainstorm ideas that would make them better: practicing, asking help from an expert, *teaching* someone else, and so on.

★ Let's Learn:
Bright comets are visible in the sky only once or twice in a century and stay visible for many days or weeks. You are far more likely to see a meteor than a comet. Meteors flash in the sky every night. Meteor flashes are sometimes called falling or shooting stars, but meteors are not stars. We see the bright flash for only a few seconds.

COMETS & METEORS

Let's Create: A Meteor Mural

★ **What You Need:**
Sponge patterns (p. 55), sponges, scissors, large roll of butcher paper, tempera paints, paint tins or trays, newsprint, glitter (optional), pins (optional), pen (optional)

★ **What You Do:**
1. Duplicate the sponge patterns to use as templates to cut out sponge shapes. For easy cutting, pin the pattern to a thin, slightly damp sponge, and cut along the line. Or trace the pattern onto the sponge with a thin, dark pen, then cut.
2. Cover the working area with newsprint.
3. Thin the tempera paint slightly, then pour just a little into a flat container or pie tin.
4. Let the children dip the sponges into the paint tins and make sponge prints on the paper. If they drag the circular sponges across the paper, they will leave a trail of paint like a comet's tail. If they dip the star patterns into the paint and press them on the paper, they can make star and constellation designs. If they drag the star patterns, they can make "shooting stars," or meteors.
5. For glittering comets and twinkling "shooting stars" mix glitter into the tempera paint, or let children shake glitter onto the finished mural. (Once the mural is dry, the excess glitter can be shaken off and saved for another activity.)
6. Post the completed mural in the room or in a hallway.

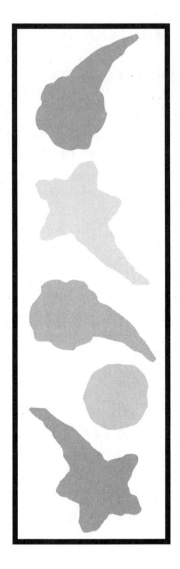

SPONGE PATTERNS

COMETS & METEORS

Let's Find Out: What a Meteor Looks Like

Discuss meteors with your children. In all likelihood they have seen a meteor but mistakenly called it a falling or shooting star. The bright flash of a meteor lasts only a few seconds.

★ What You Need:
Flashlight

★ What You Do:
1. Have the children sit together in a circle on the rug.
2. Dim the lights (or turn them off completely).
3. Let the children's eyes grow accustomed to the darkness.
4. Stand away from the circle and raise the flashlight over your head.
5. Turn the flashlight on and move it sharply downward. Then turn it off. (This should take only a second or two.)
6. Ask the children what they saw. Then have them watch the skies at night with their parents, looking for meteors.

Book Link:
• *Comets, Meteors, and Asteroids* by Seymour Simon (Morrow Junior Books, 1994). Facts and interesting color photographs to show children.

COMETS & METEORS

Let's Play: Shooting Star Board Game

★ What You Need:

Game board pattern (p. 58), marker and spinner patterns
(p. 59), crayons or felt pens, clear Contac paper, heavy
paper or oak tag, brad, scissors

★ What You Do:

1. Duplicate the game board pattern, color as desired, and
cover with clear Contac paper.
2. Duplicate the spinner onto heavy paper, color as desired,
and cut out. Do the same with the arrow.
3. Attach the arrow to the spinner loosely with the brad.
(Make sure that the arrow can turn on the brad.)
4. Duplicate the game markers onto heavy paper, color, and
cut out.
5. Explain the game to the children. When they spin the
marker, they move to the next square of the same shape. For
example, if the spinner points to a shooting star, they move to
the next square with a star picture in it. The first child to reach
the moon is the winner.

GAME BOARD PATTERN

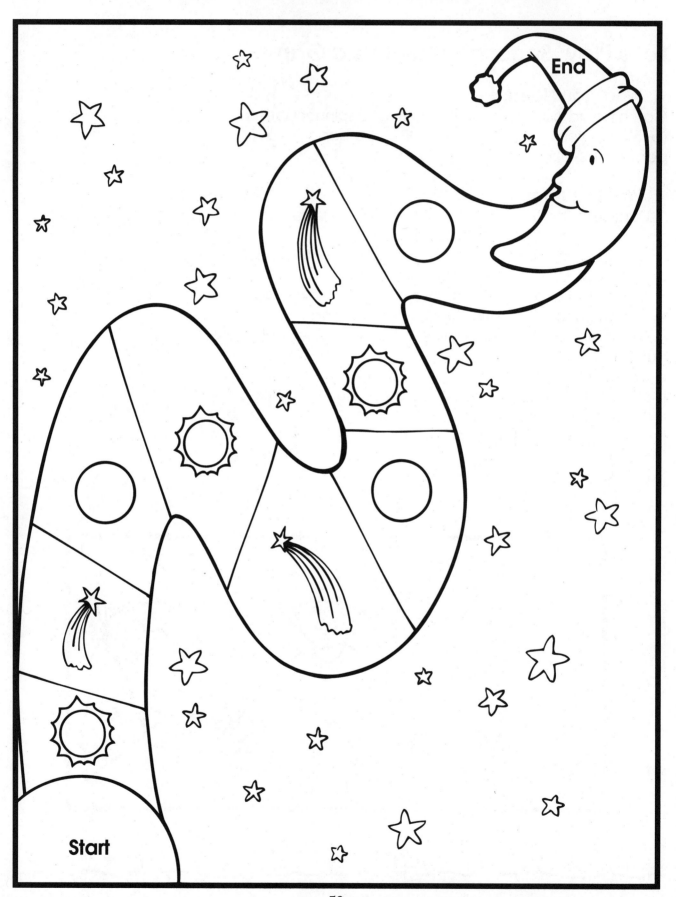

End

Start

MARKERS & SPINNER

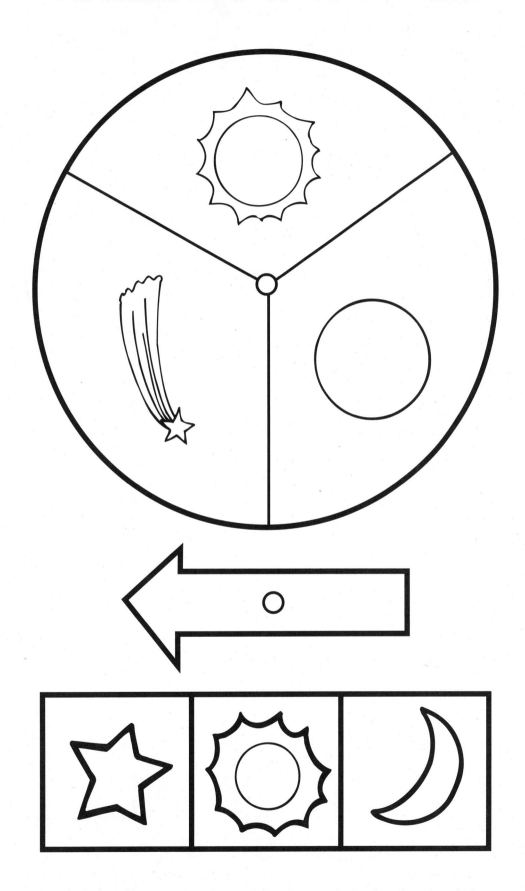

COMETS & METEORS

Let's Sing: Comet & Meteor Songs

Watch That Shooting Star
(to the tune of "Row, Row, Row Your Boat")

Watch that shooting star,
Falling from the sky!
Meteor, meteor, meteor, meteor,
Flash as you go by!

I See a Comet
(to the tune of "You Are My Sunshine")

I see a comet,
A fiery comet,
It leaves a bright trail
Across the sky.
A comet's visit,
Is just a short one,
So I will watch it,
And then wave goodbye.

Meteor
(to the tune of "This Old Man")

Meteor, in the sky,
Wink at us as you go by—
You look like a falling star,
Shooting from the sky,
Wink and blink as you go by.

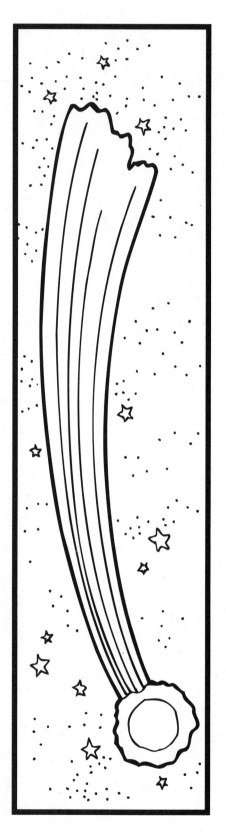

"I'M A COMET"

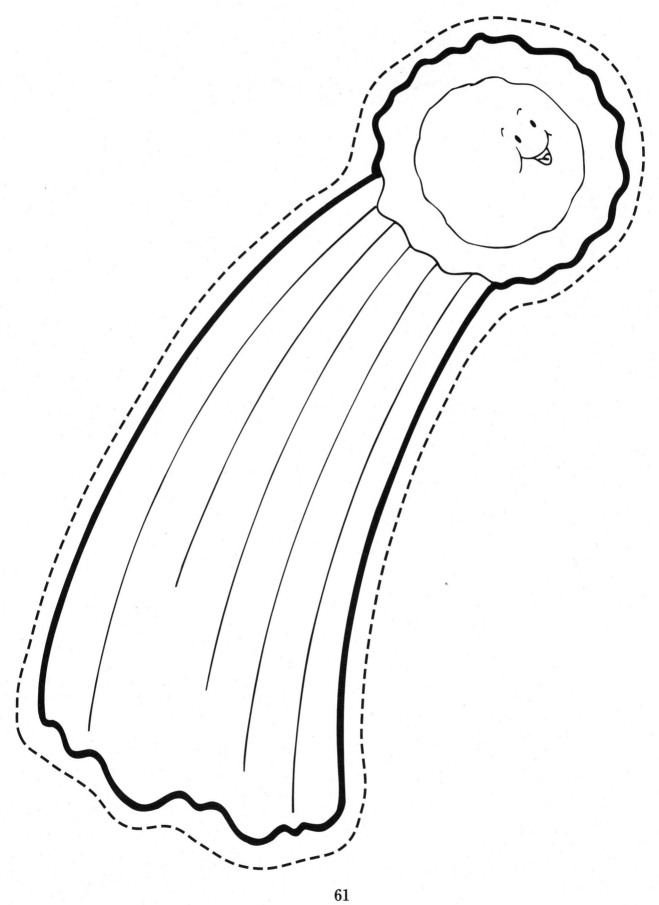

"I'M A METEOR"

ASTRONAUTS

Introduction

★ Let's Read:
Curious George Gets a Medal by H.A. Rey (Houghton Mifflin, 1957).
In this Curious George tale, George, always a curious monkey, gets in trouble at a local museum. He is forgiven (for destroying the dinosaur display) after he agrees to be the first monkey in space. George does splendidly in the ship, pulling a lever right on time and floating back down to Earth in his parachute. He even gets a medal that says: To George, the First Space Monkey.

★ Let's Talk:
Ask if any of the children has ever been the first to do something, the way George was the first space monkey in this story. Perhaps children were the first in line at the slide, or the first in their family to try a new food, and so on. Then give each child a chance to be first at something: first to water the plants in the garden, first to clean up before snack, first to go on the swings, and so on. Let children make their own medals from paper plates and gold crayons to celebrate their uniqueness.

★ Let's Learn:
On July 20, 1969, Neil Armstrong and Edwin "Buzz" Aldrin became the first men to set foot on the moon. Astronauts eat special food in space. Sometimes the food comes in tubes or plastic bags. You have to be careful when you drink in space, or the liquid will just float away!

Let's Create: My Personal Spacesuit

Curious George's spacesuit was special because it was the smallest size—perfect for the little monkey. Your children can make their spacesuits special, too.

★ What You Need:

Spacesuit pattern (p. 65), crayons or markers, aluminum foil, buttons, sequins, glitter, glue, scissors, photographs of the children (optional)

★ What You Do:

1. Duplicate the spacesuit pattern for each of your children.
2. Let the children decorate the patterns with crayons and markers.
3. Provide additional adornments, including buttons, sequins, foil, and glitter, for children to use to make their spacesuits spectacular!
4. If possible, have children bring in photographs of themselves. (Make sure these are duplicates.) Let children cut out their faces from the photos and place them in the helmet portion of the mask. These will truly personalize their pictures. (Otherwise, they can draw in their own face.)

Option: Duplicate the "Space Badge" on the astronaut page to use for name tags. Write each child's name on one of the patterns, then safety pin it to the child's clothing when going on field trips. These patterns can also be used on cubby holes or desks.

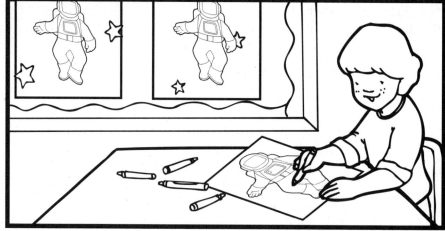

SPACESUIT PATTERN

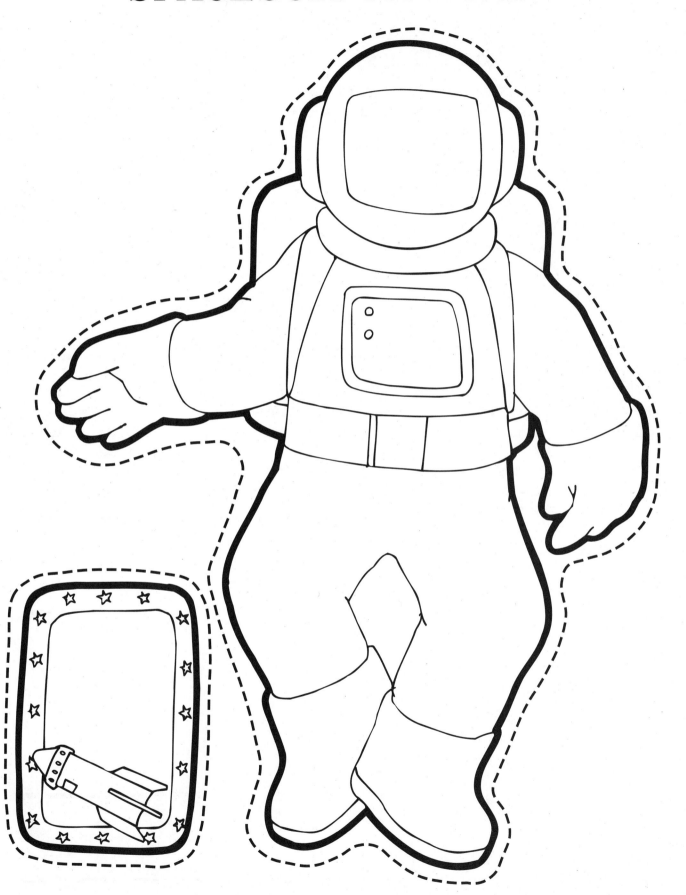

Let's Find Out: About Gravity

Discuss the concept of gravity with the children. Gravity is what keeps us from floating off Earth. In space, unless an object is fastened to something, it just floats around.

★ **What You Need:**
Scale, set of balances, items to weigh, paper, marker

★ **What You Do:**
1. Weigh each child and keep a record of the weight on a piece of paper.
2. Have children weigh small objects in a set of balances. They can see how much a pencil weighs, a crayon, a book, and so on.
3. Talk about the fact that in space, these items would not weigh anything.
4. Ask the children whether they would like to float or not. Have them imagine what it would be like on Earth if there were no gravity.

Option: Show pictures from books about astronauts, such as the one listed below, that has photographs of astronauts in space—where there is zero gravity.

Book Links:
• *Astronauts* by Carol Greene (Childrens Press, 1984). This factual book also has color photographs of astronauts.
• *Journey to the Moon* by Erich Fuchs (Delacorte, 1969). A beautifully illustrated picture book of the journey to the moon.

ASTRONAUTS

Let's Play: Blast Off! Tag

This game should be played outside.

★ What You Need:
Nothing

★ What You Do:
1. Designate one area as safe.
2. One child is "It." The other children run and hide.
3. The child who is "It" counts down from 10 or 20 to zero, employing the same method as NASA does when the rockets take off: 10, 9, 8, 7, 6, 5, 4, 3, 2, 1, BLAST OFF!
4. Then this child tries to find the others.
5. The other children try to run to the safe area, before "It" tags them.
6. The last child caught is "It" in the next round.

ASTRONAUTS

Let's Sing: Astronaut Songs

Would You Like to Fly?

(to the tune of "Do Your Ears Hang Low?")

Would you like to try
Flying rockets in the sky?
Would you like to float around?
Would your seat belt hold you down?
Do you think that you could stand
Having food fly from your hand?
Would you like to fly?

Where'd My Drink Go?

(to the tune of "Alouette")

Where'd my drink go?
Hey, where did my drink go?
Where'd my drink go?
Did it float away?
It is hard to drink in space,
Things just float around the place.
Drink in space,
Drink in space,
'Round the place,
'Round the place,
Ohhhh.
Where'd my drink go?
Hey, where did my drink go?
Where'd my drink go?
Did it float away?

"I'M AN ASTRONAUT"

SPACESHIPS

Introduction

★ Let's Read:

UFO Diary by Satoshi Kitamura (Farrar, 1989).
A UFO loses its way in space and lands on a strange blue planet where it meets and befriends a young boy. The boy shows the alien around Earth, and the alien takes the boy for a whirl in its spaceship.

★ Let's Talk:

Ask if any of the children has ever been lost. (If so, what did the child do?) Discuss things to do if someone gets lost: ask a police officer for help, go to an information center, and so on. Remind children to always make a plan when they are out with their parents, so that if anyone gets lost, they'll know where to go. (This would also be an appropriate time to discuss emergency numbers, home numbers, and addresses.)

★ Let's Learn:

Nobody knows if UFOs (or flying saucers) really exist. However, UFOs have been reported as being luminescent objects that fly or float in odd, logic-defying ways. Many alleged sightings have been explained as reflections caused by the sun on airplanes, or weather balloons, or simply different weather-related conditions. Still, some sightings remain unexplained.

SPACESHIPS

Let's Create: A Space Visitor Diary

★ **What You Need:**
Crayons or markers, paper

★ **What You Do:**
1. Give each child two sheets of paper.
2. Have the children pretend they're space visitors. Tell them they have just arrived on Earth and everything is very new to them.
3. Have the children draw a picture on one page of the most unique thing they find (as aliens) on Earth.
4. Then have the children pretend to be Earthlings visiting a foreign planet. Have them illustrate the second page as if they were tourists in outer space.
5. Bind the completed pictures together in a cooperative diary.

Option: Fold and staple small books or journals for each traveler. Make the cover out of aluminum foil for a high-tech look. Children can use plain tempera painted onto the aluminum for further decorating.

SPACESHIPS

Let's Find Out: About Flying Saucers

★ **What You Need:**
Stiff paper plates, tempera paint, paintbrushes, beads, sequins, buttons, fabric scraps, pipe cleaners, dried pasta shapes, glue, stapler, tape, film canisters, silver or gold spray paint (optional), string (optional)

★ **What You Do:**
1. Give each child two paper plates to color (the outside) using tempera paint.
2. Provide assorted decorative items for children to glue to the outside of the plates.
3. Help children attach the two plates together using glue, staples, or tape.
4. While their saucers are drying, let children decorate film canisters to look like their ideas of space visitors. (They can use paint, plus the decorative items listed above.)
5. Let children play with their saucers and space visitors.

Option 1: Spray paint the paper plates using gold or silver paint ahead of time and let dry. Let children decorate these metallic saucers. Or let children decorate the saucers with textured items, and *then* spray using metallic paint.

Option 2: Tape a length of string to the top of each saucer and hang from the ceiling or a clothesline strung across your classroom.

Let's Play: Flying Saucers

★ What You Need:
Frisbees (foam rubber disks also work well)

★ What You Do:
1. Show children how to throw a Frisbee.
2. Let children practice throwing the disks. Make sure that they are throwing them away from the rest of the children. (They will not be trying to catch them at this age, but only throwing to see how far they can make the saucers fly.)
3. Have the children observe the Frisbees in the air. These disks have flying saucer shapes.
4. Children can pretend that the Frisbees are flying saucers.

Option: Give each child a strong paper plate to color using crayons or markers. Children can make their own personal flying saucers.

Let's Play: Creature Concentration

★ What You Need:
Creature Concentration cards (p. 75), crayons or markers, scissors, clear Contac paper (optional)

★ What You Do:
1. Duplicate the patterns, color, and cut out. (Make sure that you color the two sets of each creature identically.)
2. Cover with clear Contac paper, if you'd like, and cut out again.
3. Show the children how to play the game. They turn all of the cards face-down, then flip two cards over at a time. If the cards match, they keep the set and try again. If the cards do not match, they turn them face-down and another child takes a turn.
4. The child with the most matches at the end wins.

CREATURE
CONCENTRATION CARDS

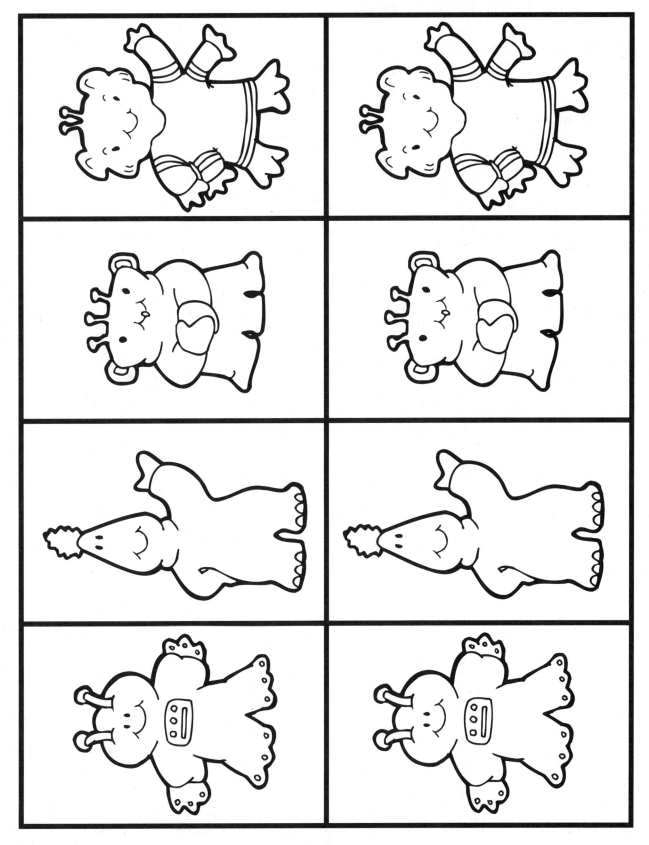

SPACESHIPS

Let's Sing: Spaceship Songs

What's That in the Sky?
(to the tune of "Row, Row, Row Your Boat)

What's that in the sky,
What's that neat machine?
UFO, UFO, UFO, UFO,
Shiny, bright, and clean.

A UFO Landed at My House
(to the tune of "My Bonnie Lies Over the Ocean")

A UFO landed at my house,
The ship was all shiny and clean.
I watched it as silent as a mouse
To see what there was to be seen (be seen).
Spaceship, oh, spaceship,
Which planet have you come from (come from)?
Spaceship, oh, spaceship,
Please tell me which planet you're from!

The Visitors Have Come from Space
(to the tune of "The Ants Go Marching One by One")

The visitors have come from space,
Hurrah, hurrah.
The visitors have come from space,
Hurrah, hurrah.
The visitors have come from space,
They're small and they're green
And they float 'round the place.
Yes, they've come from outer space,
Outer space,
In their UFO.
(Boom, boom, boom!)

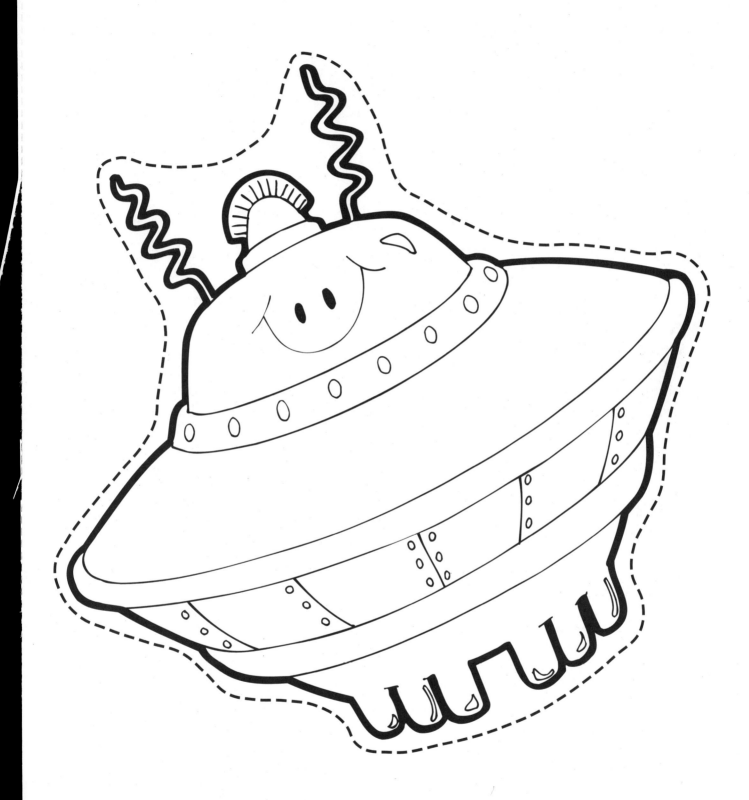

~ STORYBOOK RESOURCES ~

Stars:
- *Starbaby* by Frank Asch (Scribner's, 1980).
- *The Sun, the Moon, and the Stars* by Mae Freeman (Random House, 1979).
- *How the Stars Fell into the Sky* by Jerrie Oughton (Houghton, 1992).
- *The Night Stella Hid the Stars* by Gail Radley (Crown, 1978).
- *The Starry Sky* by Rose Wyler (Messner, 1989).

Moon:
- *Moon Song* by Byrd Baylor (Scribner's, 1982).
- *Regards to the Man in the Moon* by Ezra Jack Keats (Four Winds, 1981).
- *The Moon Jumpers* by Janice May Udry (Harper, 1959).
- *Moon Man* by Tomi Ungerer (Harper, 1967).
- *Moonfall* by Susan Whitcher, pictures by Barbara Lehman (Farrar, Straus & Giroux, 1993).

Sun:
- *Sun Up* by Alvin Tresselt, illustrated by Henri Sorensen (Lothrop, Lee & Shepard, 1991).
- *Why Mosquitoes Buzz in People's Ears: A West African Tale* by Verna Aardema (Dial, 1975). A Caldecott Award winner (1976).

Planets:
- *Ellsworth and the Cats from Mars* by Patience Brewster (Houghton Mifflin, 1981).

Astronauts:
- *I Want to Be an Astronaut* by Byron Barton (Crowell, 1988).
- *The Three Astronauts* by Umberto Eco (Harcourt, 1989).

Spaceships:
- *The Magic Rocket* by Steven Kroll (Holiday, 1992).
- *High-Noon Rocket* by Charles Paul May (Holiday, 1966).
- *Professor Noah's Spaceship* by Brian Wildsmith (Oxford University Press, 1981).

UFOs & Aliens:
- *It Came from Outerspace* by Tony Bradman (Dial, 1982).
- *Cosmic Chickens* by Ned Delaney (Harper, 1988).
- *2-B and the Space Visitor* by Sherry Paul (Childrens Press, 1981).
- *Guys from Space* by Daniel Manus Pinkwater (Macmillan, 1989).
- *UFO Kidnap* by Nancy Robison (Lothrop, 1978).

~ NONFICTION RESOURCES ~

Stars:
- *The Book of Stars for You* by Franklyn M. Branley, illustrated by Leonard Kessler (Crowell, 1967).
- *The Sky Is Full of Stars* by Franklyn M. Branley (Crowell, 1981).

Moon:
- *The Earth's Moon* by Isaac Asimov (Gareth Stevens, 1988).

Sun:
- *The Way to Start a Day* by Byrd Baylor, illustrated by Peter Parnall (Scribner's, 1978). Text and illustrations describe how people all over the world celebrate the sunrise.
- *The Sun's Family of Planets* by Allan Fowler (Childrens Press, 1992). A "Rookie Read-Aloud Science" book.
- *Exploring the Sun* by Roy A. Gallant, illustrated by Lee J. Ames (Garden City Books, 1958). For teachers' use only.
- *The Sun* by Alice Fields, illustrated by Tony Gibbons & Mike Tregenza (Franklin Watts, 1980). An Easy-Read Fact Book.
- *Sunlight and Shadows* by John and Cathleen Polgreen (Doubleday, 1967).

Planets:
- *The Planets in Our Solar System* by Franklyn M. Branley (Crowell, 1987).
- *A Book of Planets for You* by Franklyn M. Branley (Crowell, 1966).

Comets & Meteors:
- *Comets and Meteors* by George S. Fichter (Franklin Watts, 1982).

Astronauts:
- *I Can Be an Astronaut* by June Behrens (Childrens Press, 1984).
- *The Astronauts* by Dinah L. Moche (Random House, 1979).

Miscellaneous Sky Books:
- *Space Songs* by Myra Cohn Livingston, illustrated by Leonard Everett Fisher (Holiday House, 1988).
- *Sky Songs* by Myra Cohn Livingston, illustrated by Leonard Everett Fisher (Holiday House, 1984).

Periodicals:
Odyssey: Science That's Out of This World (February 1995), vol. 4, #2: "Invaders from Space: Asteroids, Meteorites, and Comets"
Cobblestone Publishing
7 School Street
Peterborough, NH 03458
10 issues for $22.95 (prices subject to change)

~ MORE MONDAY MORNING ~ RESOURCES

The "Happy World" series encourages students to explore and respect the world around them. Students will make unique crafts, read (or listen to) interesting literature links, sing songs to familiar tunes, and play great games!

Animal Friends
Gr. PreK-1, 80 pp., MM 2012

Promote concern for endangered animals through creative early learning activities. Each animal "unit" includes a pattern of the animal that can be made into a puppet, plus a face mask of the animal.

Friends from Around the World
Gr. PreK-1, 80 pp., MM 2013

Activities such as "Glitter Letters," "Feeling Concentration," "Your Passport, Please," and "Traveling 'Round and 'Round" will encourage children to become friends with people from around the world! Patterns to duplicate and enlarge will enhance classroom decor.

Art from Throwaways
Gr. PreK-1, 80 pp., MM 2014

From trash to treasure, your students will tap into their creative sides while using recyclable materials! Children will love turning milk cartons into "Yellow Submarines" and paper bags into "Wild West Vests"! Included for each project are reproducible wordless directions for students.